THE CITY OF DREADFUL NIGHT

James Thomson (1834–82), was born at Port Glasgow, the son of a merchant seaman who suffered a paralytic stroke in 1840. The family then moved to London, but Thomson's mother died within two years and the boy was sent to the Royal Caledonian Asylum for the children of indigent Scottish servicemen. He was educated there and at the Royal Military Asylum in Chelsea from where he joined the army to serve as a schoolmaster. Posted to Ireland in 1851 Thomson met Charles Bradlaugh, the publisher of the *National Reformer* which was soon to feature his work. He continued to serve in Ireland and England, but increasing bouts of depression and drinking led to dismissal from the army in 1862. He returned to London to seek a career in literature and journalism, and continued his studies in French, German and Italian. Thomson chose the pseudonym 'B.V.' (Bysshe Vanolis) because of his admiration for Shelley and the eighteenth-century German romantic poet Novalis.

In the early 1870s Thomson worked as secretary to a mine company in Colorado, and as war correspondent in Spain for the *New York World*. None of these jobs lasted very long and he did not find it easy to get his creative work published. Thomson's greatest achievement, *The City of Dreadful Night*, dates from 1874 when it appeared in instalments for the *National Reformer*. When published in book form with further poems in 1880, its deeply pessimistic vein did not go down well with most reviewers, although George Eliot and George Meredith were admirers. A further collection of poems appeared that year, and Thomson's other writings appeared in *Essays and Phantasies* (1881) and *Satires and Profanities* (1884). Increasingly addicted to alcohol, Thomson's last years were close to penury, until a final drinking bout sent him to University College Hospital London where he died of an internal haemorrhage in 1882. He is buried in Highgate Cemetery.

JAMES THOMSON

THE
CITY OF
DREADFUL
NIGHT

INTRODUCED
BY EDWIN MORGAN

CANONGATE
CLASSICS
53

First published in Great Britain in 1880 by Reeves & Turner
& Dobell. First published as a Canongate Classic in 1993
by Canongate Press Ltd, 14 Frederick Street, Edinburgh
EH2 2HB. Introduction and Notes © Edwin Morgan 1993.
All rights reserved.

British Library Cataloguing-in-Publication Data
A catalogue record for this book is available on request
from the British Library.

ISBN 0 86241 449 0

CANONGATE CLASSICS
Series Editor: Roderick Watson
Editorial Board: Tom Crawford, J. B. Pick

The publishers gratefully acknowledge general subsidy from
the Scottish Arts Council towards the Canongate Classics
series and a specific grant towards the publication of this title.

Set in Plantin by Dalrymple
Printed and bound in Great Britain
by Biddles, Guildford, Surrey

Contents

Introduction

'The most anticipative poem of his time' is how Edmund
Blunden described *The City of Dreadful Night* in his 1932
selection of Thomson's poetry. Whatever its shifting
status may have been among literary critics, it is certainly
a poem of notable and sometimes surprising reverbera-
tions. Rudyard Kipling read it when he was still at school
and tells in his autobiography (*Something of Myself*, 1937)
how it 'shock me to my unformed core'. Later, working
as a young journalist in Lahore, he used his own nocturnal insomniac wanderings through Lahore's streets as a
Thomsonian analogy in his story '"The City of Dreadful
Night"', which is permeated with verbal echoes of
Thomson's poem. Jack London's *The People of the Abyss*
(1903), an account of his experience of slum life in the
East End of London during the previous year, shows
how Thomson's title had already become common cur-
rency in its references to 'The City of Dreadful Monotony' – an idea not foreign to the original poem. T. S.
Eliot freely admitted the strong influence Thomson's
poem had had on him when he began to write, and that
influence clearly left its marks on *The Waste Land*, not
only through urban imagery but in philosophical and
religious ideas as well. (There is a good discussion of
the relation between Thomson and Eliot in Robert
Crawford, *The Savage and the City in the Work of T. S.
Eliot*, Oxford, 1987, chap. 2.) And more recently, John
Rechy's novel *City of Night* (1963), a saga of homosexual
hustling in the streets of New York and other American
cities, sets down its epigraph from Thomson: 'The City
is of Night; perchance of Death, / But certainly of Night.'
Rechy's appropriation of the poem suggests a new

subtext for the 'sad Fraternity' of the Proem, and its statement that 'None uninitiate by many a presage / Will comprehend the language of the message.'

The potency of this poem, wherever it comes from and however one describes it, is not really in doubt. Counter-arguments based on its rhetorical language, or its pessimistic content, have to face that fact. If Thomson's reputation has been uncertain, it is tempting to relate this to his being an uprooted Scot living in other places, i.e. is he a Scottish or an English writer, and does it matter? Similar uncertainties have attended the reputations of Carlyle and Stevenson, of John Davidson, of Robert Buchanan and David Gray. It could be argued – has been argued – that in Victorian times Scottish literature suffered from this hiving off of talent (even if the talent is minor, as with Buchanan and Gray), but taken from the point of view of the writers themselves, the question is how easy or difficult it was for a Scottish poet brought up in or migrating to England at that period to write persuasively in English, considering the fact that his antecedents in Scotland were Fergusson, Burns, and Hogg. And if it was difficult, were there nevertheless compensating advantages? The whole change of environment from Scotland to (say) London – the complex of physical, cultural, linguistic changes – may also have forced, under pressure of various kinds, new ways of looking at things, a new awareness of things that an outsider suddenly sees and points out. T. S. Eliot's published tribute to both Thomson and Davidson – perhaps as an incomer himself he was all the more receptive – was that they had a particular kind of modernity, a sort of prophetic modern adumbration, deeply incorporating urban experience into poetry, which he did not find in their English contemporaries. The two Scottish poets were alienated, whether psychologically or geographically or both, and their lives may fairly be called tragic, but Eliot swept his eye over them more widely and saw them as figures symbolic of the exile and alienation of the early-modern artist.

But who or what alienated Thomson? What made him an alcoholic, an atheist, a pessimist, and are these three quite separate conditions? An early editor and biographer, Bertram Dobell, called him the 'laureate of pessimism', and the dubious accolade has not helped enlightenment. Certainly his life was not short of disappointment, frustration, grief. As a child, he saw a much loved younger sister die 'of measles caught from me'. He was brought up mostly in institutions. He was 'discharged with disgrace' from the army. His mining company in America collapsed. He was recalled from the war in Spain as an incompetent reporter. He may, though the facts are wanting, have loved an adolescent girl who died young. His literary work, though highly appreciated by some, did not bring him widespread fame. Towards the end, despite the attempts of friends to look after him, he drank more and more heavily, disappeared for long periods, sometimes in prison, sometimes living on the streets, sleeping in model lodging-houses or just walking about all night. When he was dying he dragged himself to the house of a friend, the blind poet Philip Bourke Marston, and terrified the helpless man by haemorrhaging on his couch. The dreadful nights of the poem are not absent from the life. His last words, according to William Sharp who heard them, were at once so desperate and so defiant that he did not dare to record them.

Whether such personal disasters and guilts are foreground or background, the whole picture would doubtless include the move from Scotland to England, the influence of Darwinism on matters of faith, his acquaintance over many years with the militant atheist Charles Bradlaugh, and the whole modern complex of reactions to living in the mass society of a huge city. Yet

to call him the 'laureate of pessimism' is a curiously mis-
leading piece of shorthand. Thomson was far from being
a gloomy or dull man. He was a lively talker; he loved
children and got on well with them; some of his poems,
like 'Sunday up the River' and 'Sunday at Hampstead',
are light lyrical tributes to the open air, to picnics and
holidays and groups of bantering young friends and lovers. He enjoyed – and it is quite a list – boating, fishing,
swimming, horse-riding, grouse-shooting, sleighing,
singing, playing poker, dancing quadrilles, playing the
clarinet, going to concerts and operas, games of tennis,
games of billiards – yes, it is all documented, many non-
dreadful nights and days. In his literary criticism, which
often shows great insight, he praised Burns, Blake,
Shelley, Rabelais, Browning, and above all Walt
Whitman – writers who have either a fine sense of com-
edy or a positive, enjoying, forward-looking attitude to
life. He had his own darker favourites, like Leopardi and
Heine, both of whom he translated, but he did not rec-
ommend them at the expense of more optimistic spirits.
He was, in fact, a man of unusually wide culture, and
although his essays and articles and reviews were mostly
published in relatively obscure periodicals like the
National Reformer and *Cope's Tobacco Plant* (a trade jour-
nal in Liverpool with literary leanings – and Thomson
being a heavy and enthusiastic smoker was the perfect
contributor!), you discover when you read them that he
was often more in touch with contemporary develop-
ments than (say) Matthew Arnold who, in his essays on
modern or recent writers, had a genius for picking out
the second-rate or simply not knowing what was really
going on in Europe or America, whereas Thomson did
know, and he read and translated from French, German
and Italian. Thomson was one of the first people in
Britain to see the importance of Blake, of Leopardi, of
Whitman and Melville, of Stendhal and Flaubert; he

admired Edgar Allan Poe; he was interested (as an opium-taker himself, though apparently not a habitual one) in the drug culture of De Quincey and Baudelaire and he referred admiringly to Baudelaire's *Les Paradis artificiels*. He loved Beethoven and Mozart and knew their music intimately.

This man of many accomplishments, and many desperations, is seen chiefly as a poet, and although his prose works are certainly recommended reading, it is his poetry which projects itself most strongly. It is very uneven; some of it has tremendous power, some of it is turgid, loose, over-adjectival, trying too hard. Poems of note include 'In the Room', a macabre piece in which various items of furniture speak about the man who has lived in the room and who now lies dead on the bed, having poisoned himself; 'Low Life', a poem of social comment in the tradition of Thomas Hood's 'Song of the Shirt' and John Davidson's 'Thirty Bob a Week', giving the conversation of a sempstress overheard on a train; 'A Real Vision of Sin', a sort of manic horror story 'written in disgust at Tennyson's ['The Vision of Sin'], which is very pretty and clever and silly and truthless' as his headnote tells us; and poems in praise of Burns and Blake, the latter showing a particular relevance to Thomson himself, and to London:

> He came to the desert of London Town
> > Grey miles long;
> He wandered up and he wandered down,
> > Singing a quiet song ...

Some longer poems – 'The Doom of a City', 'To Our Ladies of Death', 'Insomnia' – have close links with *The City of Dreadful Night*, as does the prose piece (it could be called a prose-poem), 'A Lady of Sorrow', with which he opened the volume of his *Essays and Phantasies* (1881). This last, an impressive meditation on the 'night-side of nature', influenced by Novalis's *Hymns to the Night* (which Thomson had translated) and probably by Leopardi's more philosophical poems, contains many of the themes and images of *The City of Dreadful Night* – the brotherhood, the dead girl, the statue of the woman, the fossils from prehistory, and above all 'the City, the vast Metropolis which was become as a vast Necropolis, desolate as a Pariah'. 'The Doom of a City' is an early, pre-atheist fantasy which goes on much too long but has some powerful scenes, in particular the vision of a City of the Dead where the inhabitants are petrified and the sea is frozen:

> Dim stony merchants holding forth rich wares
> To catch the choice of purchasers of stone;
> Fair statues leaning over balconies,
> Whose bosoms made the bronze and marble chill;
> Statues about the lawns, beneath the trees;
> Firm sculptured horsemen on stone horses still;
> Statues fixed gazing on the flowing river
> Over the bridge's sculptured parapet;
> Statues in boats, amidst its sway and quiver
> Immovable as if in ice-waves set.

'Insomnia', one of his last poems, is also one of his most remarkable. As an attempt to convey a state of mind through imagery and through analogies of physical action, it has outstanding force and dedication. Basically, as its blunt title suggests, it presents a realistic underpinning of *The City of Dreadful Night*. The speaker of the poem goes to bed at midnight, cannot sleep, counts the hours till five a.m., puts on his clothes, goes out and walks the streets till daybreak, finally returns to his 'homeless home'. The approach of each of the night hours is signalled by the appearance of a dark shrouded figure; these relentless Watchers have furled wings which they could only unfurl if the speaker fell asleep. The space between each of the hours, the fearfully stretched sense of time which insomnia gives, is evoked by having the would-be sleeper climb painfully down one sharp-rocked, root-snarled wall of a ravine and equally pain-fully up the wall at the other side, 'the night before me an immense / Black waste of ridge-walls, hour by hour apart.' The transition from this level of reality, which one would call 'nightmarish' if the sleepless man would not in fact have relished a real nightmare, to the one-degree-more-real reality of the streets, mediated verbally though it is, is highly effective.

> Against a bridge's stony parapet
>   I leaned, and gazed into the waters black;
> And marked an angry morning red and wet
>   Beneath a livid and enormous rack
> Glare out confronting the belated moon,
> Huddled and wan and feeble as the swoon
>   Of featureless Despair:
> When some stray workman, half-asleep but lusty,
> Passed urgent through the rainpour wild and gusty,
> I felt a ghost already, planted watching there.

The workman is pure Leopardi, but fits perfectly into the London setting. 'Half-asleep' is masterly, focusing the theme of the poem by its contrast between the 'lusty' yawning man rushing to his early work after a night's sleep and the 'ghostly' insomniac whose purposelessness hovers from house to street to house. Flaws like 'waters black' and 'moon / swoon' do not disappear, but seem to become part of a voice one has learned to place some trust in; that is the way he does things; that is him.

The City of Dreadful Night, written between 1870 and 1874, is a well-constructed poem which is all the more impressive as it appears to have taken its origin in some psychological crisis. A diary entry for 4 November, 1869 shows Thomson making a bonfire of 'all my old papers, manuscripts, and letters' in what he calls a 'sad and stupid' mood. He refers to his climacteric thirty-fifth birthday in that month, but there is more to it than that. 'But after this terrible year, I could do no less than consume the past.' Why 1869 was 'terrible', no one has been able to explain, but that fact, dealt with in one sense by the burning of the papers, and in another by his acknowledgement of standing at a watershed ('35 on the 23rd inst.'), seems to have released the inspirational floodgates: at the beginning of 1870 he started work on *The City of Dreadful Night*. Perhaps it is not surprising that he took his first epigraph from Dante, who also at the age of thirty-five found himself in a dark wood where the way ahead was lost. Thomson's dark wood certainly included insomnia; in a letter to George Eliot (20 June, 1874) he described the poem as 'the outcome of much sleepless hypochondria', and a letter to his sister-in-law Julia (9 April, 1880) warned her it was one of several poems 'written under evil inspiration of insomnia'. The poem may have come out of a crisis, but many things culminate in it.

In accordance with its title, the whole poem deals with or takes place in a city at night. Passages of general comment alternate with passages describing action as the speaker wanders through different parts of the city and has various meetings and encounters. It is not any actual city, though it is certainly based on London, and possibly incorporates some of Thomson's early memories of Glasgow and Port Glasgow. But he makes it clear that it is not to be identified: it has 'great ruins of an unremembered past', which is not London, and the landscape to the north of it is a wilderness of mountains and savannahs which has been influenced by his travels in America (especially Colorado) and possibly Spain (the Pyrenees). So it becomes simply 'the city', any city that is very large and very old, it has huge buildings, great bridges, squares, cathedrals, mansions, slums, endless streetlamps. Since it is night, the streets are relatively empty, but because it is a large city there are plenty of shadowy nocturnal wanderers who are the inhabitants of the place and the actors of the poem – the outcasts of daytime society, the tramps, the drunks, the drug-addicts, the half-crazed, the homeless, the sleepless, the lonely. The poem emphasises the isolation of all these characters: they murmur to themselves, they creep about wrapped up in their own thoughts, they appear as products of a dehumanising process in society which is becoming so competitive it has no room for failure; there are also of course psychological weaknesses which are not being blamed on society, but they too take their place within the parameters that society sets up, and the individual seems able to do less and less to change his condition. The speaker, the 'I' of the poem, who is clearly a projection of Thomson himself, is both an inhabitant of this night world, a familiar, an intimate, who can align himself with its sufferings, and yet also an observer, an artist, a reporter, an imaginative reconstructor, who is able to stand apart and build up a poem, an art object, for an audience. Thomson keeps the poem moving forward by the alternation of abstract and particular passages, and works everything towards a strong conclusion, with an added special effect which seems deliberate. In Section II the speaker describes how he follows a man who shows him three spots in the city where in his experience Faith, Love, and Hope died one after the other, and the speaker is horrified when he discovers that in this walk they have come round in a circle, and that his companion (like someone in Dante's *Inferno*) is about to proceed on his way again in an endless haunting of his own sense of loss. 'He circled thus for ever tracing out / The series of the fraction left of Life; / Perpetual recurrence in the scope / Of but three terms, dead Faith, dead Love, dead Hope.' And Thomson's footnote explains that he is thinking in mathematical terms:

Life divided by that persistent three $= \dfrac{\text{LXX}}{333} = .\overset{.}{2}1\overset{.}{0}.$

Now this recurring decimal, this 'Perpetual recurrence', applies also to the poem itself. The 210 refers to the 21 sections of the poem plus the introduction or 'Proem'. So in reading the poem you are setting off on a circular journey, and the last stanza loops back to the first, catching you in a trap like the inhabitants of the city. These opening and closing stanzas have the same rhymes, except that the slightly hopeful 'there / air / fair' of the beginning has become the 'air / there / despair' of the end. Thomson not only admired Dante, who has similar effects, but was knowledgeable in mathematics; at school, indeed, he had better marks for mathematics than for English.

The main problem in the poem was how to avoid monotony, since the characters are in a state of withdrawal from life, and the poem is about the difficulty of escaping from a despairing state of mind. Some monotony is required, simply to bring home to the reader the awful repetitiveness of such lives, the sense of being on a treadmill. Yet the poem must also be to some extent striking, strange, dramatic; it has to move forward somehow. Critical opinions have differed on this, but I believe Thomson has managed the matter rather well, and introduced sufficient variety without destroying the overall mood or tone. Much of the poem is like a nightmare, or a series of nightmares, from the unhappy fitful sleep of an insomniac. There are images of terror or desolation or destruction, often reminiscent of Edgar Allan Poe and looking forward to the Surrealists. Thomson makes the obvious point that in this nocturnal city there is normally no traffic, but suddenly, in Section IX, the speaker hears a great rumble of wheels and 'the trampling clash of heavy ironshod feet', and a huge carriage, loaded, groaning, with snorting straining horses, rolls past and disappears into the night again – unexplained, a sudden image of fear, a portent of something unknown. In Section IV

a speaker (not the speaker of the poem) stands in a
square and addresses an imaginary crowd, telling them
about his experiences in coming through a terrible desert
where he was attacked by monstrous creatures, in scenes
reminiscent of Hieronymus Bosch, or some of the illus-
trations of Gustave Doré.

> As I came through the desert thus it was,
> As I came through the desert: Lo you, there,
> That hillock burning with a brazen glare;
> Those myriad dusky flames with points a-glow
> Which writhed and hissed and darted to and fro;
> A Sabbath of the Serpents, heaped pell-mell
> For Devil's roll-call and some *fête* of Hell:
>> Yet I strode on austere;
>> No hope could have no fear.

As in Eliot's *The Waste Land*, images of desert and city
are often combined by Thomson, emphasising a theme
of static sterility, and often (as in Eliot) connected with
sex. In a late autobiographical letter to his sister-in-law
Julia (1882) he ended by saying he had been 'Ishmael in
the desert from my childhood.' The Ishmael character in
the desert of Section IX, though only observed, is there-
fore strongly identified with by Thomson. After the passage just quoted, the desert wanderer sees a woman with
a red oil-dripping lamp in her hand, and as he comes
closer he realises it is in fact her heart that she is carrying.
He splits into two selves, one self bent over beside the
woman who tries to wipe away from his face the blood
that drops from her heart / lamp, the other self standing
watching, in agony, unable to move, until eventually the
woman and the first self are swept away by a sea and he
is left alone, half of himself, an outcast, and forced like
the Ancient Mariner to tell and retell the story. The idea
of the split self is not only something that reminds us of
'doubles' in Hoffmann, Hogg, Poe, and Stevenson, but
something that has a painful relevance to Thomson him-

self. A good friend of his called Jack Barrs told Henry Salt (Thomson's biographer) how greatly his drinking bouts disturbed his personality:

> His absolute abandonment during these attacks was sufficient to attest their nature, and no more pregnant illustration of the metamorphosis he underwent could well be found than the remark made by his landlord's children on one such occasion. Thomson was naturally very loving with children, and children invariably returned his affection. Once, when he came back to his rooms in Huntley Street in the fulness of the change wrought by his excesses, the children went to the door to admit him, but closed it again and went to their father, telling him that 'Mr. Thomson's wicked brother was at the door'; and for some time they could not recognise 'our Mr. Thomson' in the figure of the dipsomaniac claiming his name. (H. S. Salt, *The Life of James Thomson*, 1905, p.128)

The melodrama latent in good brother and wicked brother, or in the split selves of the Ishmael character in the desert, does of course burst out fully in the image of the woman carrying her dripping heart, and there is a stagy or Gothick element in several scenes in the poem, as open to criticism or defence as similar things in Edgar Allan Poe, where the defence is surely that extreme and nightmarish states of mind are being presented as vividly as possible. In Section X the speaker of the poem goes into a large mansion which has all its windows blazing with light; inside, everything is covered with black, every room has a little shrine with candles and a picture or a bust of a young girl, and in one room the dead girl herself is laid out, with a young man kneeling beside her. This is all very artificial, yet it has the logical artificiality of a dream, even the realism of a dream; it is like a carefully devised scene from a Cocteau film. At any rate, erotic guilt and sterility are certainly one of the recurring themes, whether or not we are meant to link this with the alienations of modern urbanised society. In one of the strangest passages of the poem, the short Section VII, the speaker suggests that there are phantoms as well as human beings in the city, phantoms mingling with men – he has seen them – from beyond the grave, *like* men but more shameless, less secretive:

> And yet a man who raves, however mad,
>> Who bares his heart and tells of his own fall,
> Reserves some inmost secret good or bad:
>> The phantoms have no reticence at all:
> The nudity of flesh will blush though tameless,
> The extreme nudity of bone grins shameless,
>> The unsexed skeleton mocks shroud and pall.

This is a curious mixture of the medieval Dance of Death and something very modern in its expression of fascination with the idea of the loss of sexual shame.

But we are not meant to forget that this a poem about the loss of God, or the death of God, and it includes, in one of its main scenes, in Section XIV, an anti-sermon preached in a cathedral: various night people drift about the pews or slump by the walls, and the rather impressive man in the pulpit tells them that at least they have only one life to endure – there is no God – man as a species will die out eventually, like the mammoth – he preaches a doctrine of stoic necessity:

> I find no hint throughout the Universe
> Of good or ill, of blessing or of curse;
>> I find alone Necessity Supreme.

These various human figures that Thomson uses – the man who had come through the desert, the woman carrying her heart, the young man in the big house with the dead girl, the rugged preacher in the cathedral – may be said to culminate in the grim figure presented in Section XVIII. The speaker of the poem goes to the north of the city (and in Christian iconography the north is 'bad', the north of Heaven is where Satan gathered his legions to attack God); he comes to a triple fork of lanes, with damp trees and heavy white mist (the *three* suggesting important choice, like the three paths in the ballad of *Thomas Rymer*); he chooses one and walks gingerly down it until he hears and vaguely sees something crawling and sobbing, thinks it is perhaps a wounded animal – 'The hind limbs stretched to push, the fore limbs then / To drag' – but finds it is a man, or what 'had been a man', wounded indeed at hands and knees but ready to wound others with poisoned blade and sulphuric phial. The mixture of wild menace and pitiable condition initiates a drama where each man fears the other. The crawling man fears that the intruder has come to snatch his secret, since he has tried the other two lanes and is now sure that he is on the right track to find the gold he has been searching for – but this is fool's gold, it is 'the long-lost broken golden thread / Which reunites my present with my past'. The image of the filthy, bleeding, angry, mad old man dragging himself through a ditch below a hedge in search of the long-gone innocence of childhood –

> From this accursed night without a morn,
>   And through the deserts which have else no track,
>   And through vast wastes of horror-haunted time,
> To Eden innocence in Eden's clime:
>
> And I become a nursling soft and pure,
>   An infant cradled on its mother's knee,
>   Without a past, love-cherished and secure...

– is both shocking and moving in a way that makes it hard not to think of Samuel Beckett. But Thomson has his own subtle touch. As the speaker leaves the scene he has to brush off some 'thin shreds of gossamer' from his face – thin, but more real than the thin threads of gold the other man will never find.

In the last two sections, the human figures (apart

from the observer) fall away in favour of more symbolic figures, statues and images, as if to stress the freezing of all real meaningful human activity in the city. In Section XX the speaker sits leaning against a column in the forecourt of a large cathedral; in front of him are two great statues, facing one another: a sphinx, and an angel with a sword, the angel staring hard at the sphinx but the sphinx staring only into its own time and space. The speaker is drowsy, and nods off three times, being wakened each time by a loud crash, as the stone wings, the stone sword, and finally the whole stone angel fall and shatter. The cold moonlight has now come round and lies full on the awesome expressionless face of the unchanged sphinx. If the guardian angel, the militant angel, the angel with the sword is no longer able to protect the city, the city must resign itself to being in the hands of fate. Thomson's sphinx seems to be Egyptian rather than Greek, simple, enormous, ancient, a 'couchant' lion with a human face and a blank gaze. There is so much 'desert' in Thomson's poems that it is not strange to come across a sphinx, a creature neither protective nor inimical, an indifferent node of power and law which cannot be appealed to or questioned or in any way altered but which the speaker describes as 'grand' and 'majestic' and which appears to have the function of reminding human beings that they belong to a universe and not just a city or a world. The space that the sphinx stares into is void but infinite. It suggests far thoughts. The speaker does not switch off. He 'pondered long', in Shelleyan mood. What was out there?

Section XXI, the last section, takes us again to the north of the city, where there is a bleak ridge or plateau, a badlands we might call it, and on the ridge a colossal bronze statue of a winged, seated woman who is based on the figure in Albrecht Dürer's well-known engraving *Melencolia I* (1514). With her folded, unused wings, she

is the presiding deity or patron saint of the night city, the
embodiment of whatever it is that makes the night city
dreadful. Mainly it is an image of lethargy and apathy;
she sits with her cheek in her hand, gazing at nothing,
surrounded by objects of knowledge and science, books,
mathematical instruments, tools, scales, an hour-glass.
In her melancholy she is abstracted from all the arts and
sciences which (if she could rouse herself) she has the full
power to make use of. She is static, frozen, waiting, like
the petrified people in 'The Doom of a City'. Her melancholy is not feeble, or plangent, or even sad. There is a
suggestion of great endurance and patience, great latent
force, a force that remains under an even more forceful
spell, and so cannot act in the real world. Motionless
herself, she suffers an illusion, a beautiful illusion, of
coming alive under the motions of the heavenly bodies:

The moving moon and stars from east to west

Circle before her in the sea of air;

Shadows and gleams glide round her solemn rest.

But nothing happens; the spell is not broken; the night
is still the night.

In that final section, although it deals thematically
with the domination of the sense of being trapped, the
sense of despair, there are many words which seem to
give a countering impression of trying to find or establish
values: words like 'titanic', 'sombre', 'sublimity', 'solemn', 'stern', 'heroic'. One of the qualities the poem
does have is a certain majestic effect, a kind of cumula-
tive grandeur which comes not so much from any resolu-
tion of the ideas as from the artist's successful wrestling
with his material: by the end he really has established his
city, it is an image in our minds, a 'place of the mind' in
Tom Leonard's phrase, an image both archetypal and
modern. When he was putting finishing touches to the
poem early in 1874, he wrote in a diary entry (4 April,
1874):

> Wet, coldish morning. Not up till past one o'clock.
> Wet all day. Then wrote away at Whitman, finishing
> in a fashion draught of biographical sketch, as well as
> going through last two parts of 'City of Night'.
> Walked with Fred before and after dinner. Walked
> self after tea. Imagination deeply stirred.

That last phrase is a key to the reality, to the strength, to
the strangeness of the poem. It is a work of the creative
imagination, whatever it may owe to London or to
Thomson's life or to Dante and Leopardi and Novalis,
and our imaginations when we read it are also 'deeply
stirred'. This – the making of non-art into art – is what
gives a poem containing such massive negatives an overall positive. Leopardi in his notebooks (*Zibaldone*, 259–
260), aware of being regarded as a 'pessimist', made the
point once and for all:

> Works of genius have the intrinsic property, that even
> when they give a perfect likeness of the nullity of
> things ... even when they express the most terrible
> despair ... always serve as a consolation, rekindling
> enthusiasm, and though speaking of and portraying
> nothing but death, restore to it, at least for a while,
> the life that it had lost. (Leopardi, *Moral Tales*, trans.
> Patrick Creagh, Manchester, 1983)

It may well be that the negatives in Thomson's 'City'
would not have been quickened so readily into artistic
life if he himself had not had a genuine interest in the
phenomenon of the large modern city, and indeed if he
had not had a range of responses to the phenomenon. It
is of some note that in the diary entry of 1874 quoted
above, he in finishing *The City of Dreadful Night* at the
same time as he is writing about Walt Whitman, a poet
he much admired. In that Whitman essay, published in
the *National Reformer* in 1874, he says:

> He sings with boundless elation the cities of his nur-
> ture, New York and Brooklyn; the superb Manahatta,

planted on her fish-shaped island, with the North
River and the East River and the ocean flashing
around her busy wharves; the great cosmopolitan city
with her fierce teeming passionate life, her industries,
her splendours, and her crimes.

That of course is New York, and it is a part of his excited
stimulated reaction to America in general. London was
no doubt different. In a fragment of prose written in
1872, he expressed through images but very clearly just
how alienated he felt as he wandered about London:

> The isolation of thought is sometimes almost appall-
> ing. Walking in the streets at night and sunk in mus-
> ing, I come up to the surface and regard the moving
> people; and they seem to me distant and apparently
> unrelated as ships on the horizon traversing the ocean
> between unknown foreign ports; and there are mo-
> ments when they seem incalculably and inconceivably
> remote, as stars and star systems in infinite space.
> (*Poems, Essays and Fragments*, ed. J. M. Robertson,
> 1892, p.261)

Total alienation! And yet, as in the poem, what you
notice in reading the passage is how his (and your)
imagination is wonderfully stirred, and you cannot wish
him to have been other than he was, 'walking in the
streets at night and sunk in musing'.

EDWIN MORGAN

THE CITY
OF DREADFUL NIGHT

Per me si va nella città dolente.

DANTE

Poi di tanto adoprar, di tanti moti
D'ogni celeste, ogni terrena cosa,
Girando senza posa,
Per tornar sempre là donde son mosse;
Uso alcuno, alcun frutto
Indovinar non so.

Sola nel mondo eterna, a cui si volve
Ogni creata cosa,
In te, morte, si posa
Nostra ignuda natura;
Lieta no, ma sicura
Dell' antico dolor ...
Però ch' esser beato
Nega ai mortali e nega a' morti il fato.

LEOPARDI

Melencolia I (1514) by Albrecht Dürer

PROEM

Lo, thus, as prostrate, 'In the dust I write
   My heart's deep languor and my soul's sad tears.'
Yet why evoke the spectres of black night
   To blot the sunshine of exultant years?
Why disinter dead faith from mouldering hidden?   5
Why break the seals of mute despair unbidden,
   And wail life's discords into careless ears?

Because a cold rage seizes one at whiles
   To show the bitter old and wrinkled truth
Stripped naked of all vesture that beguiles,   10
   False dreams, false hopes, false masks and modes of youth;
Because it gives some sense of power and passion
In helpless impotence to try to fashion
   Our woe in living words howe'er uncouth.

Surely I write not for the hopeful young,   15
   Or those who deem their happiness of worth,
Or such as pasture and grow fat among
   The shows of life and feel nor doubt nor dearth,
Or pious spirits with a God above them
To sanctify and glorify and love them,   20
   Or sages who foresee a heaven on earth.

For none of these I write, and none of these
   Could read the writing if they deigned to try:
So may they flourish, in their due degrees,
   On our sweet earth and in their unplaced sky.   25
If any cares for the weak words here written,
It must be some one desolate, Fate-smitten,
   Whose faith and hope are dead, and who would die.

Yes, here and there some weary wanderer
    In that same city of tremendous night,   30
Will understand the speech, and feel a stir
    Of fellowship in all-disastrous fight;
'I suffer mute and lonely, yet another
Uplifts his voice to let me know a brother
    Travels the same wild paths though out of sight.'   35

O sad Fraternity, do I unfold
    Your dolorous mysteries shrouded from of yore?
Nay, be assured; no secret can be told
    To any who divined it not before:
None uninitiate by many a presage   40
Will comprehend the language of the message,
    Although proclaimed aloud for evermore.

I

The City is of Night; perchance of Death,
    But certainly of Night; for never there
Can come the lucid morning's fragrant breath
    After the dewy dawning's cold grey air:
The moon and stars may shine with scorn or pity;   5
The sun has never visited that city,
    For it dissolveth in the daylight fair.

Dissolveth like a dream of night away;
    Though present in distempered gloom of thought
And deadly weariness of heart all day.   10
    But when a dream night after night is brought
Throughout a week, and such weeks few or many
Recur each year for several years, can any
    Discern that dream from real life in aught?

For life is but a dream whose shapes return,   15
    Some frequently, some seldom, some by night
And some by day, some night and day: we learn,
    The while all change and many vanish quite,
In their recurrence with recurrent changes
A certain seeming order; where this ranges   20
    We count things real; such is memory's might.

A river girds the city west and south,
    The main north channel of a broad lagoon,
Regurging with the salt tides from the mouth;
    Waste marshes shine and glister to the moon   25
For leagues, then moorland black, then stony ridges;
Great piers and causeways, many noble bridges,
    Connect the town and islet suburbs strewn.

Upon an easy slope it lies at large,
    And scarcely overlaps the long curved crest   30
Which swells out two leagues from the river marge.
    A trackless wilderness rolls north and west,
Savannahs, savage woods, enormous mountains,
Bleak uplands, black ravines with torrent fountains;
    And eastward rolls the shipless sea's unrest.   35

The city is not ruinous, although
    Great ruins of an unremembered past,
With others of a few short years ago
    More sad, are found within its precincts vast.
The street-lamps always burn; but scarce a casement   40
In house or palace front from roof to basement
    Doth glow or gleam athwart the mirk air cast.

The street-lamps burn amidst the baleful glooms,
    Amidst the soundless solitudes immense
Of rangèd mansions dark and still as tombs.   45
    The silence which benumbs or strains the sense
Fulfils with awe the soul's despair unweeping:
Myriads of habitants are ever sleeping,
    Or dead, or fled from nameless pestilence!

Yet as in some necropolis you find   50
    Perchance one mourner to a thousand dead,
So there; worn faces that look deaf and blind
    Like tragic masks of stone. With weary tread,
Each wrapt in his own doom, they wander, wander,
Or sit foredone and desolately ponder   55
    Through sleepless hours with heavy drooping head.

Mature men chiefly, few in age or youth,
    A woman rarely, now and then a child:
A child! If here the heart turns sick with ruth
    To see a little one from birth defiled,   60
Or lame or blind, as preordained to languish
Through youthless life, think how it bleeds with anguish
    To meet one erring in that homeless wild.

They often murmur to themselves, they speak
    To one another seldom, for their woe   65
Broods maddening inwardly and scorns to wreak
    Itself abroad; and if at whiles it grow
To frenzy which must rave, none heeds the clamour,
Unless there waits some victim of like glamour,
    To rave in turn, who lends attentive show.   70

The City is of Night, but not of Sleep;
    There sweet sleep is not for the weary brain;
The pitiless hours like years and ages creep,
    A night seems termless hell. This dreadful strain
Of thought and consciousness which never ceases,   75
Or which some moments' stupor but increases,
    This, worse than woe, makes wretches there insane.

They leave all hope behind who enter there:
    One certitude while sane they cannot leave,
One anodyne for torture and despair;   80
    The certitude of Death, which no reprieve
Can put off long; and which, divinely tender,
But waits the outstretched hand to promptly render
    That draught whose slumber nothing can bereave.[1]

[1] Though the Garden of thy Life be wholly waste, the
    sweet flowers withered, the fruit-trees barren, over its wall
    hang ever the rich dark clusters of the Vine of Death,
    within easy reach of thy hand, which may pluck of them
    when it will.

I I

Because he seemed to walk with an intent
    I followed him; who, shadowlike and frail,
Unswervingly though slowly onward went,
    Regardless, wrapt in thought as in a veil:
Thus step for step with lonely sounding feet   5
We travelled many a long dim silent street.

At length he paused: a black mass in the gloom,
    A tower that merged into the heavy sky;
Around, the huddled stones of grave and tomb:
    Some old God's-acre now corruption's sty: 10
He murmured to himself with dull despair,
Here Faith died, poisoned by this charnel air.

Then turning to the right went on once more,
    And travelled weary roads without suspense;
And reached at last a low wall's open door,   15
    Whose villa gleamed beyond the foliage dense:
He gazed, and muttered with a hard despair,
Here Love died, stabbed by its own worshipped pair.

Then turning to the right resumed his march,
    And travelled street and lanes with wondrous strength,   20
Until on stooping through a narrow arch
    We stood before a squalid house at length:
He gazed, and whispered with a cold despair,
Here Hope died, starved out in its utmost lair.

When he had spoken thus, before he stirred,   25
    I spoke, perplexed by something in the signs
Of desolation I had seen and heard
    In this drear pilgrimage to ruined shrines:
When Faith and Love and Hope are dead indeed,
Can Life still live? By what doth it proceed?   30

As whom his one intense thought overpowers,
    He answered coldly, Take a watch, erase
The signs and figures of the circling hours,
    Detach the hands, remove the dial-face;
The works proceed until run down; although   35
Bereft of purpose, void of use, still go.

Then turning to the right paced on again,
    And traversed squares and travelled streets whose glooms
Seemed more and more familiar to my ken;
    And reached that sullen temple of the tombs;   40
And paused to murmur with the old despair,
Here Faith died, poisoned by this charnel air.

I ceased to follow, for the knot of doubt
    Was severed sharply with a cruel knife:
He circled thus for ever tracing out   45
    The series of the fraction left of Life;
Perpetual recurrence in the scope
Of but three terms, dead Faith, dead Love, dead Hope.[1]

[1] Life divided by that persistent three $= \dfrac{\text{LXX}}{333} = .\dot{2}1\dot{0}.$

[33]

III

Although lamps burn along the silent streets,
    Even when moonlight silvers empty squares
The dark holds countless lanes and close retreats;
    But when the night its sphereless mantle wears
The open spaces yawn with gloom abysmal,   5
The sombre mansions loom immense and dismal,
    The lanes are black as subterranean lairs.

And soon the eye a strange new vision learns:
    The night remains for it as dark and dense,
Yet clearly in this darkness it discerns   10
    As in the daylight with its natural sense;
Perceives a shade in shadow not obscurely,
Pursues a stir of black in blackness surely,
    Sees spectres also in the gloom intense.

The ear, too, with the silence vast and deep   15
    Becomes familiar though unreconciled;
Hears breathings as of hidden life asleep,
    And muffled throbs as of pent passions wild,
Far murmurs, speech of pity or derision;
But all more dubious than the things of vision,   20
    So that it knows not when it is beguiled.

No time abates the first despair and awe,
    But wonder ceases soon; the weirdest thing
Is felt least strange beneath the lawless law
    Where Death-in-Life is the eternal king;   25
Crushed impotent beneath this reign of terror,
Dazed with such mysteries of woe and error,
    The soul is too outworn for wondering.

I V

He stood alone within the spacious square
    Declaiming from the central grassy mound,
With head uncovered and with streaming hair,
    As if large multitudes were gathered round:
A stalwart shape, the gestures full of might,   5
The glances burning with unnatural light: –

As I came through the desert thus it was,
As I came through the desert: All was black,
In heaven no single star, on earth no track;
A brooding hush without a stir or note,   10
The air so thick it clotted in my throat;
And thus for hours; then some enormous things
Swooped past with savage cries and clanking wings:
    But I strode on austere;
    No hope could have no fear.   15

As I came through the desert thus it was,
As I came through the desert: Eyes of fire
Glared at me throbbing with a starved desire;
The hoarse and heavy and carnivorous breath
Was hot upon me from deep jaws of death;   20
Sharp claws, swift talons, fleshless fingers cold
Plucked at me from the bushes, tried to hold:
    But I strode on austere;
    No hope could have no fear.

As I came through the desert thus it was,   25
As I came through the desert: Lo you, there,
That hillock burning with a brazen glare;
Those myriad dusky flames with points a-glow
Which writhed and hissed and darted to and fro;
A Sabbath of the Serpents, heaped pell-mell   30
For Devil's roll-call and some *fête* of Hell:
    Yet I strode on austere;
    No hope could have no fear.

As I came through the desert thus it was,
As I came through the desert: Meteors ran   35
And crossed their javelins on the black sky-span;
The zenith opened to a gulf of flame,
The dreadful thunderbolts jarred earth's fixed frame;
The ground all heaved in waves of fire that surged
And weltered round me sole there unsubmerged: 40
    Yet I strode on austere;
    No hope could have no fear.

As I came through the desert thus it was,
As I came through the desert: Air once more,
And I was close upon a wild sea-shore;   45
Enormous cliffs arose on either hand,
The deep tide thundered up a league-broad strand;
White foambelts seethed there, wan spray swept and flew;
The sky broke, moon and stars and clouds and blue:
    Yet I strode on austere;   50
    No hope could have no fear.

As I came through the desert thus it was,
As I came through the desert: On the left
The sun arose and crowned a broad crag-cleft;
There stopped and burned out black, except a rim,   55
A bleeding eyeless socket, red and dim;
Whereon the moon fell suddenly south-west,
And stood above the right-hand cliffs at rest:
    Yet I strode on austere;
    No hope could have no fear.   60

As I came through the desert thus it was,
As I came through the desert: From the right
A shape came slowly with a ruddy light;
A woman with a red lamp in her hand,
Bareheaded and barefooted on that strand;   65
O desolation moving with such grace!
O anguish with such beauty in thy face!
    I fell as on my bier,
    Hope travailed with such fear.

As I came through the desert thus it was,   70
As I came through the desert: I was twain,
Two selves distinct that cannot join again;
One stood apart and knew but could not stir,
And watched the other stark in swoon and her;
And she came on, and never turned aside,   75
Between such sun and moon and roaring tide:
    And as she came more near
    My soul grew mad with fear.

As I came through the desert thus it was,
As I came through the desert: Hell is mild   80
And piteous matched with that accursèd wild;
A large black sign was on her breast that bowed,
A broad black band ran down her snow-white shroud;
That lamp she held was her own burning heart,
Whose blood-drops trickled step by step apart: 85
    The mystery was clear;
    Mad rage had swallowed fear.

As I came through the desert thus it was,
As I came through the desert: By the sea
She knelt and bent above that senseless me;   90
Those lamp-drops fell upon my white brow there,
She tried to cleanse them with her tears and hair;
She murmured words of pity, love, and woe,
She heeded not the level rushing flow:
    And mad with rage and fear,   95
    I stood stonebound so near.

As I came through the desert thus it was,
As I came through the desert: When the tide
Swept up to her there kneeling by my side,
She clasped that corpse-like me, and they were borne   100
Away, and this vile me was left forlorn;
I know the whole sea cannot quench that heart,
Or cleanse that brow, or wash those two apart:
    They love; their doom is drear,
    Yet they nor hope nor fear;   105
    But I, what do I here?

V

How he arrives there none can clearly know;
    Athwart the mountains and immense wild tracts,
Or flung a waif upon that vast sea-flow,
    Or down the river's boiling cataracts:
To reach it is as dying fever-stricken;   5
To leave it, slow faint birth intense pangs quicken;
    And memory swoons in both the tragic acts.

But being there one feels a citizen;
    Escape seems hopeless to the heart forlorn:
Can Death-in-Life be brought to life again?   10
    And yet release does come; there comes a morn
When he awakes from slumbering so sweetly
That all the world is changed for him completely,
    And he is verily as if new-born.

He scarcely can believe the blissful change,   15
    He weeps perchance who wept not while accurst;
Never again will he approach the range
    Infected by that evil spell now burst:
Poor wretch! who once hath paced that dolent city
Shall pace it often, doomed beyond all pity,   20
    With horror ever deepening from the first.

Though he possess sweet babes and loving wife,
    A home of peace by loyal friendships cheered,
And love them more than death or happy life,
    They shall avail not; he must dree his weird;   25
Renounce all blessings for that imprecation,
Steal forth and haunt that builded desolation,
    Of woe and terrors and thick darkness reared.

VI

I sat forlornly by the river-side,
    And watched the bridge-lamps glow like golden stars
Above the blackness of the swelling tide,
    Down which they struck rough gold in ruddier bars;
And heard the heave and plashing of the flow   5
Against the wall a dozen feet below.

Large elm-trees stood along that river-walk;
    And under one, a few steps from my seat,
I heard strange voices join in stranger talk,
    Although I had not heard approaching feet: 10
These bodiless voices in my waking dream
Flowed dark words blending with the sombre stream: –

And you have after all come back; come back.
I was about to follow on your track.
And you have failed: our spark of hope is black.   15

That I have failed is proved by my return:
The spark is quenched, nor ever more will burn,
But listen; and the story you shall learn.

I reached the portal common spirits fear,
And read the words above it, dark yet clear,   20
'Leave hope behind, all ye who enter here:'

And would have passed in, gratified to gain
That positive eternity of pain,
Instead of this insufferable inane.

A demon warder clutched me, Not so fast;   25
First leave your hopes behind! – But years have passed
Since I left all behind me, to the last:

You cannot count for hope, with all your wit,
This bleak despair that drives me to the Pit:
How could I seek to enter void of it?   30

He snarled, What thing is this which apes a soul,
And would find entrance to our gulf of dole
Without the payment of the settled toll?

Outside the gate he showed an open chest:
Here pay their entrance fees the souls unblest;   35
Cast in some hope, you enter with the rest.

This is Pandora's box; whose lid shall shut,
And Hell-gate too, when hopes have filled it; but
They are so thin that it will never glut.

I stood a few steps backwards, desolate;   40
And watched the spirits pass me to their fate,
And fling off hope, and enter at the gate.

When one casts off a load he springs upright,
Squares back his shoulders, breathes with all his might,
And briskly paces forward strong and light: 45

But these, as if they took some burden, bowed;
The whole frame sank; however strong and proud
Before, they crept in quite infirm and cowed.

And as they passed me, earnestly from each
A morsel of his hope I did beseech,   50
To pay my entrance; but all mocked my speech.

Not one would cede a tittle of his store,
Though knowing that in instants three or four
He must resign the whole for evermore.

So I returned. Our destiny is fell;   55
For in this Limbo we must ever dwell,
Shut out alike from Heaven and Earth and Hell.

The other sighed back, Yea; but if we grope
With care through all this Limbo's dreary scope,
We yet may pick up some minute lost hope;   60

And, sharing it between us, entrance win,
In spite of fiends so jealous for gross sin:
Let us without delay our search begin.

VII

Some say that phantoms haunt those shadowy streets,
    And mingle freely there with sparse mankind;
And tell of ancient woes and black defeats,
    And murmur mysteries in the grave enshrined:
But others think them visions of illusion,   5
Or even men gone far in self-confusion;
    No man there being wholly sane in mind.

And yet a man who raves, however mad,
    Who bares his heart and tells of his own fall,
Reserves some inmost secret good or bad: 10
    The phantoms have no reticence at all:
The nudity of flesh will blush though tameless,
The extreme nudity of bone grins shameless,
    The unsexed skeleton mocks shroud and pall.

I have seen phantoms there that were as men   15
    And men that were as phantoms flit and roam;
Marked shapes that were not living to my ken,
    Caught breathings acrid as with Dead Sea foam:
The City rests for man so weird and awful,
That his intrusion there might seem unlawful,   20
    And phantoms there may have their proper home.

VIII

While I still lingered on that river-walk,
  And watched the tide as black as our black doom,
I heard another couple join in talk,
  And saw them to the left hand in the gloom
Seated against an elm bole on the ground,   5
Their eyes intent upon the stream profound.

'I never knew another man on earth
  But had some joy and solace in his life,
  Some chance of triumph in the dreadful strife:
My doom has been unmitigated dearth.'   10

'We gaze upon the river, and we note
The various vessels large and small that float,
Ignoring every wrecked and sunken boat.'

'And yet I asked no splendid dower, no spoil
  Of sway or fame or rank or even wealth;   15
  But homely love with common food and health,
And nightly sleep to balance daily toil.'

'This all-too humble soul would arrogate
Unto itself some signalising hate
From the supreme indifference of Fate!'   20

'Who is most wretched in this dolorous place?
  I think myself; yet I would rather be
  My miserable self than He, than He
Who formed such creatures to His own disgrace.

'The vilest thing must be less vile than Thou   25
   From whom it had its being, God and Lord!
   Creator of all woe and sin! abhorred,
Malignant and implacable! I vow

'That not for all Thy power furled and unfurled,
   For all the temples to Thy glory built,   30
   Would I assume the ignominious guilt
Of having made such men in such a world.'

'As if a Being, God or Fiend, could reign,
At once so wicked, foolish, and insane,
As to produce men when He might refrain!   35

'The world rolls round for ever like a mill;
It grinds out death and life and good and ill;
It has no purpose, heart or mind or will.

'While air of Space and Time's full river flow
The mill must blindly whirl unresting so: 40
It may be wearing out, but who can know?

'Man might know one thing were his sight less dim;
That it whirls not to suit his petty whim,
That it is quite indifferent to him.

'Nay, does it treat him harshly as he saith?   45
It grinds him some slow years of bitter breath,
Then grinds him back into eternal death.'

I X

It is full strange to him who hears and feels,
  When wandering there in some deserted street,
The booming and the jar of ponderous wheels,
  The trampling clash of heavy ironshod feet:
Who is this Venice of the Black Sea rideth?   5
Who in this city of the stars abideth
  To buy or sell as those in daylight sweet?

The rolling thunder seems to fill the sky
  As it comes on; the horses snort and strain,
The harness jingles, as it passes by;   10
  The hugeness of an overburthened wain:
A man sits nodding on the shaft or trudges
Three parts asleep beside his fellow-drudges:
  And so it rolls into the night again.

What merchandise? whence, whither, and for whom?   15
  Perchance it is a Fate-appointed hearse,
Bearing away to some mysterious tomb
  Or Limbo of the scornful universe
The joy, the peace, the life-hope, the abortions
Of all things good which should have been our portions, 20
  But have been strangled by that City's curse.

X

The mansion stood apart in its own ground;
    In front thereof a fragrant garden-lawn,
High trees about it, and the whole walled round:
    The massy iron gates were both withdrawn;
And every window of its front shed light,   5
Portentous in that City of the Night.

But though thus lighted it was deadly still
    As all the countless bulks of solid gloom;
Perchance a congregation to fulfil
    Solemnities of silence in this doom,   10
Mysterious rites of dolour and despair
Permitting not a breath of chant or prayer?

Broad steps ascended to a terrace broad
    Whereon lay still light from the open door;
The hall was noble, and its aspect awed,   15
    Hung round with heavy black from dome to floor;
And ample stairways rose to left and right
Whose balustrades were also draped with night.

I paced from room to room, from hall to hall,
    Nor any life throughout the maze discerned;   20
But each was hung with its funereal pall,
    And held a shrine, around which tapers burned,
With picture or with statue or with bust,
All copied from the same fair form of dust:

A woman very young and very fair; 25
    Beloved by bounteous life and joy and youth,
And loving these sweet lovers, so that care
    And age and death seemed not for her in sooth:
Alike as stars, all beautiful and bright,
These shapes lit up that mausoléan night. 30

At length I heard a murmur as of lips,
    And reached an open oratory hung
With heaviest blackness of the whole eclipse;
    Beneath the dome a fuming censer swung;
And one lay there upon a low white bed, 35
With tapers burning at the foot and head:

The Lady of the images: supine,
    Deathstill, lifesweet, with folded palms she lay:
And kneeling there as at a sacred shrine
    A young man wan and worn who seemed to pray: 40
A crucifix of dim and ghostly white
Surmounted the large altar left in night: –

The chambers of the mansion of my heart,
In every one whereof thine image dwells,
Are black with grief eternal for thy sake. 45

The inmost oratory of my soul,
Wherein thou ever dwellest quick or dead,
Is black with grief eternal for thy sake.

I kneel beside thee and I clasp the cross,
With eyes for ever fixed upon that face,   50
So beautiful and dreadful in its calm.

I kneel here patient as thou liest there;
As patient as a statue carved in stone,
Of adoration and eternal grief.

While thou dost not awake I cannot move;   55
And something tells me thou wilt never wake,
And I alive feel turning into stone.

Most beautiful were Death to end my grief,
Most hateful to destroy the sight of thee,
Dear vision better than all death or life.   60

But I renounce all choice of life or death,
For either shall be ever at thy side,
And thus in bliss or woe be ever well. –

He murmured thus and thus in monotone,
    Intent upon that uncorrupted face,   65
Entranced except his moving lips alone:
    I glided with hushed footsteps from the place.
This was the festival that filled with light
That palace in the City of the Night.

XI

What men are they who haunt these fatal glooms,
　　And fill their living mouths with dust of death,
And make their habitations in the tombs,
　　And breathe eternal sighs with mortal breath,
And pierce life's pleasant veil of various error　　　　5
To reach that void of darkness and old terror
　　Wherein expire the lamps of hope and faith?

They have much wisdom yet they are not wise,
　　They have much goodness yet they do not well,
(The fools we know hàve their own Paradise,　　　　10
　　The wicked also have their proper Hell);
They have much strength but still their doom is stronger,
Much patience but their time endureth longer,
　　Much valour but life mocks it with some spell.

They are most rational and yet insane:　　　　15
　　An outward madness not to be controlled;
A perfect reason in the central brain,
　　Which has no power, but sitteth wan and cold,
And sees the madness, and foresees as plainly
The ruin in its path, and trieth vainly　　　　20
　　To cheat itself refusing to behold.

And some are great in rank and wealth and power,
　　And some renowned for genius and for worth;
And some are poor and mean, who brood and cower
　　And shrink from notice, and accept all dearth　　　　25
Of body, heart and soul, and leave to others
All boons of life: yet these and those are brothers,
　　The saddest and the weariest men on earth.

XII

Our isolated units could be brought
    To act together for some common end?
For one by one, each silent with his thought,
    I marked a long loose line approach and wend
Athwart the great cathedral's cloistered square,   5
And slowly vanish from the moonlit air.

Then I would follow in among the last:
    And in the porch a shrouded figure stood,
Who challenged each one pausing ere he passed,
    With deep eyes burning through a blank white hood: 10
Whence come you in the world of life and light
To this our City of Tremendous Night? –

From pleading in a senate of rich lords
For some scant justice to our countless hordes
Who toil half-starved with scarce a human right: 15
I wake from daydreams to this real night.

From wandering through many a solemn scene
Of opium visions, with a heart serene
And intellect miraculously bright:
I wake from daydreams to this real night.   20

From making hundreds laugh and roar with glee
By my transcendent feats of mimicry,
And humour wanton as an elfish sprite:
I wake from daydreams to this real night.

From prayer and fasting in a lonely cell,   25
Which brought an ecstasy ineffable
Of love and adoration and delight:
I wake from daydreams to this real night.

From ruling on a splendid kingly throne
A nation which beneath my rule has grown   30
Year after year in wealth and arts and might:
I wake from daydreams to this real night.

From preaching to an audience fired with faith
The Lamb who died to save our souls from death,
Whose blood hath washed our scarlet sins wool-white: 35
I wake from daydreams to this real night.

From drinking fiery poison in a den
Crowded with tawdry girls and squalid men,
Who hoarsely laugh and curse and brawl and fight:
I wake from daydreams to this real night.   40

From picturing with all beauty and all grace
First Eden and the parents of our race,
A luminous rapture unto all men's sight:
I wake from daydreams to this real night.

From writing a great work with patient plan   45
To justify the ways of God to man,
And show how ill must fade and perish quite:
I wake from daydreams to this real night.

From desperate fighting with a little band
Against the powerful tyrants of our land,   50
To free our brethren in their own despite:
I wake from daydreams to this real night.

Thus, challenged by that warder sad and stern,
    Each one responded with his countersign,
Then entered the cathedral; and in turn   55
    I entered also, having given mine;
But lingered near until I heard no more,
And marked the closing of the massive door.

XIII

Of all things human which are strange ad wild
    This is perchance the wildest and most strange,
And showeth man most utterly beguiled,
    To those who haunt that sunless City's range;
That he bemoans himself for aye, repeating   5
How Time is deadly swift, how life is fleeting,
    How naught is constant on the earth but change.

The hours are heavy on him and the days;
    The burden of the mouths he scarce can bear;
And often in his secret soul he prays   10
    To sleep through barren periods unaware,
Arousing at some longed-for date of pleasure;
Which having passed and yielded him small treasure,
    He would outsleep another term of care.

Yet in his marvellous fancy he must make   15
    Quick wings for Time, and see it fly from us;
This Time which crawleth like a monstrous snake,
    Wounded and slow and very venomous;
Which creeps blindwormlike round the earth and ocean,
Distilling poison at each painful motion,   20
    And seems condemned to circle ever thus.

And since he cannot spend and use aright
    The little time here given him in trust,
But wasteth it in weary undelight
    Of foolish toil and trouble, strife and lust,   25
He naturally claimeth to inherit
The everlasting Future, that his merit
    May have full scope; as surely is most just.

O length of the intolerable hours,
    O nights that are as aeons of slow pain,   30
O Time, too ample for our vital powers,
    O Life, whose woeful vanities remain
Immutable for all of all our legions
Through all the centuries and in all the regions,
    Not of your speed and variance *we* complain.   35

We do not ask a longer term of strife,
    Weakness and weariness and nameless woes;
We do not claim renewed and endless life
    When this which is our torment here shall close,
An everlasting conscious inanition!   40
We yearn for speedy death in full fruition,
    Dateless oblivion and divine repose.

XIV

Large glooms were gathered in the mighty fane,
    With tinted moongleams slanting here and there;
And all was hush: no swelling organ-strain,
    No chant, no voice or murmuring of prayer;
No priests came forth, no tinkling censers fumed,   5
And the high altar space was unillumed.

Around the pillars and against the walls
    Leaned men and shadows; others seemed to brood
Bent or recumbent in secluded stalls.
    Perchance they were not a great multitude   10
Save in that city of so lonely streets
Where one may count up every face he meets.

All patiently awaited the event
    Without a stir or sound, as if no less
Self-occupied, doomstricken while attent.   15
    And then we heard a voice of solemn stress
From the dark pulpit, and our gaze there met
Two eyes which burned as never eyes burned yet:

Two steadfast and intolerable eyes
    Burning beneath a broad and rugged brow;   20
The head behind it of enormous size.
    And as black fir-groves in a large wind bow,
Our rooted congregation, gloom-arrayed,
By that great sad voice deep and full were swayed: –

O melancholy Brothers, dark, dark, dark!
O battling in black floods without an ark!
   O spectral wanderers of unholy Night!
My soul hath bled for you these sunless years,
With bitter blood-drops running down like tears:
   Oh dark, dark, dark, withdrawn from joy and light!   30

My heart is sick with anguish for your bale;
Your woe hath been my anguish; yea, I quail
   And perish in your perishing unblest.
And I have searched the highths and depths, the scope
Of all our universe, with desperate hope   35
   To find some solace for your wild unrest.

And now at last authentic word I bring,
Witnessed by every dead and living thing;
   Good tidings of great joy for you, for all:
There is no God; no Fiend with names divine   40
Made us and tortures us; if we must pine,
   It is to satiate no Being's gall.

It was the dark delusion of a dream,
That living Person conscious and supreme,
   Whom we must curse for cursing us with life;   45
Whom we must curse because the life He gave
Could not be buried in the quiet grave,
   Could not be killed by poison or by knife.

This little life is all we must endure,
The grave's most holy peace is ever sure,   50
   We fall asleep and never wake again;
Nothing is of us but the mouldering flesh,
Whose elements dissolve and merge afresh
   In earth, air, water, plants, and other men.

We finish thus; and all our wretched race   55
Shall finish with its cycle, and give place
   To other beings, with their own time-doom:

Infinite aeons ere our kind began;
Infinite aeons after the last man
    Has joined the mammoth in earth's tomb and womb.   60

We bow down to the universal laws,
Which never had for man a special clause
    Of cruelty or kindness, love or hate:
If toads and vultures are obscene to sight,
If tigers burn with beauty and with might,   65
    Is it by favour or by wrath of Fate?

All substance lives and struggles evermore
Through countless shapes continually at war,
    By countless interactions interknit:
If one is born a certain day on earth,   70
All times and forces tended to that birth,
    Not all the world could change or hinder it.

I find no hint throughout the Universe
Of good or ill, of blessing or of curse;
    I find alone Necessity Supreme;   75
With infinite Mystery, abysmal, dark,
Unlighted ever by the faintest spark
    For us the flitting shadows of a dream.

O Brothers of sad lives! they are so brief;
A few short years must bring us all relief: 80
    Can we not bear these years of labouring breath?
But if you would not this poor life fulfil,
Lo, you are free to end it when you will,
    Without the fear of waking after death. –

The organ-like vibrations of his voice   85
    Thrilled through the vaulted aisles and died away;
The yearning of the tones which bade rejoice
    Was sad and tender as a requiem lay:
Our shadowy congregation rested still
As brooding on that 'End it when you will.'   90

X V

Wherever men are gathered, all the air
    Is charged with human feeling, human thought;
Each shout and cry and laugh, each curse and prayer,
    Are into its vibrations surely wrought;
Unspoken passion, wordless meditation,   5
Are breathed into it with our respiration;
    It is with our life fraught and overfraught.

So that no man there breathes earth's simple breath,
    As if alone on mountains or wide seas;
But nourishes warm life or hastens death   10
    With joys and sorrows, health and foul disease,
Wisdom and folly, good and evil labours,
Incessant of his multitudinous neighbours;
    He in his turn affecting all of these.

That City's atmosphere is dark and dense,   15
    Although not many exiles wander there,
With many a potent evil influence,
    Each adding poison to the poisoned air;
Infections of unutterable sadness,
Infections of incalculable madness,   20
    Infections of incurable despair.

XVI

Our shadowy congregation rested still,
  As musing on that message we had heard
And brooding on that 'End it when you will;'
  Perchance awaiting yet some other word;
When keen as lightning through a muffled sky   5
Sprang forth a shrill and lamentable cry: –

The man speaks sooth, alas! the man speaks sooth:
  We have no personal life beyond the grave;
There is no God; Fate knows nor wrath nor ruth:
  Can I find here the comfort which I crave?   10

In all eternity I had one chance,
  One few years' term of gracious human life:
The splendours of the intellect's advance,
  The sweetness of the home with babes and wife;

The social pleasures with their genial wit;   15
  The fascination of the worlds of art,
The glories of the worlds of nature, lit
  By large imagination's glowing heart;

The rapture of mere being, full of health;
  The careless childhood and the ardent youth,   20
The strenuous manhood winning various wealth,
  The reverend age serene with life's long truth:

All the sublime prerogatives of Man;
  The storied memories of the times of old,
The patient tracking of the world's great plan   25
  Through sequences and changes myriadfold.

This chance was never offered me before;
    For me this infinite Past is blank and dumb:
This chance recurreth never, nevermore;
    Blank, blank for me the infinite To-come.   30

And this sole chance was frustrate from my birth,
    A mockery, a delusion; and my breath
Of noble human life upon this earth
    So racks me that I sigh for senseless death.

My wine of life is poison mixed with gall,   35
    My noonday passes in a nightmare dream,
I worse than lose the years which are my all:
    What can console me for the loss supreme?

Speak not of comfort where no comfort is,
    Speak not at all: can words make foul things fair?   40
Our life's a cheat, our death a black abyss:
    Hush and be mute envisaging despair. –

This vehement voice came from the northern aisle
    Rapid and shrill to its abrupt harsh close;
And none gave answer for a certain while,   45
    For words must shrink from these most wordless woes;
At last the pulpit speaker simply said,
With humid eyes and thoughtful drooping head: –

My Brother, my poor Brothers, it is thus;
This life itself holds nothing good for us,   50
    But it ends soon and nevermore can be;
And we knew nothing of it ere our birth,
And shall know nothing when consigned to earth:
    I ponder these thoughts and they comfort me.

XVII

How the moon triumphs through the endless nights!
　　How the stars throb and glitter as they wheel
Their thick processions of supernal lights
　　Around the blue vault obdurate as steel!
And men regard with passionate awe and yearning　　　　5
The mighty marching and the golden burning,
　　And think the heavens respond to what they feel.

Boats gliding like dark shadows of a dream,
　　Are glorified from vision as they pass
The quivering moonbridge on the deep black stream;　　10
　　Cold windows kindle their dead glooms of glass
To restless crystals; cornice, dome, and column
Emerge from chaos in the splendour solemn;
　　Like faëry lakes gleam lawns of dewy grass.

With such a living light these dead eyes shine,　　　　15
　　These eyes of sightless heaven, that as we gaze
We read a pity, tremulous, divine,
　　Or cold majestic scorn in their pure rays:
Fond man! they are not haughty, are not tender;
There is no heart or mind in all their splendour,　　　　20
　　They thread mere puppets all their marvellous maze.

If we could near them with the flight unflown,
　　We should but find them worlds as sad as this,
Or suns all self-consuming like our own
　　Enringed by planet worlds as much amiss:　　　　25
They wax and wane through fusion and confusion;
The spheres eternal are a grand illusion,
　　The empyréan is a void abyss.

XVIII

I wandered in a suburb of the north,
    And reached a spot whence three close lanes led down,
Beneath thick trees and hedgerows winding forth
    Like deep brook channels, deep and dark and lown:
The air above was wan with misty light,   5
The dull grey south showed one vague blur of white.

I took the left-hand lane and slowly trod
    Its earthen footpath, brushing as I went
The humid leafage; and my feet were shod
    With heavy languor, and my frame downbent,   10
With infinite sleepless weariness outworn,
So many nights I thus had paced forlorn.

After a hundred steps I grew aware
    Of something crawling in the lane below;
It seemed a wounded creature prostrate there   15
    That sobbed with pangs in making progress slow,
The hind limbs stretched to push, the fore limbs then
To drag; for it would die in its own den.

But coming level with it I discerned
    That it had been a man; for at my tread   20
It stopped in its sore travail and half-turned,
    Leaning upon its right, and raised its head,
And with the left hand twitched back as in ire
Long grey unreverend locks befouled with mire.

A haggard filthy face with bloodshot eyes,   25
    An infamy for manhood to behold.
He gasped all trembling, What, you want my prize?
    You leave, to rob me, wine and lust and gold
And all that men go mad upon, since you
Have traced my sacred secret of the clue?   30

You think that I am weak and must submit;
    Yet I but scratch you with this poisoned blade,
And you are dead as if I clove with it
    That false fierce greedy heart. Betrayed! betrayed!
I fling this phial if you seek to pass,   35
And you are forthwith shrivelled up like grass.

And then with sudden change, Take thought! take thought!
    Have pity on me! it is mine alone.
If you could find, it would avail you naught;
    Seek elsewhere on the pathway of your own: 40
For who of mortal or immortal race
The lifetrack of another can retrace?

Did you but know my agony and toil!
    Two lanes diverge up yonder from this lane;
My thin blood marks the long length of their soil;   45
    Such clue I left, who sought my clue in vain:
My hands and knees are worn both flesh and bone;
I cannot move but with continual moan.

But I am in the very way at last
    To find the long-lost broken golden thread   50
Which unites my present with my past,
    If you but go your own way. And I said,
I will retire as soon as you have told
Whereunto leadeth this lost thread of gold.

And so you know it not! he hissed with scorn;   55
    I feared you, imbecile! It leads me back
From this accursed night without a morn,
    And through the deserts which have else no track,
And through vast wastes of horror-haunted time,
To Eden innocence in Eden's clime: 60

And I become a nursling soft and pure,
    An infant cradled on its mother's knee,
Without a past, love-cherished and secure;
    Which if it saw this loathsome present Me,
Would plunge its face into the pillowing breast,   65
And scream abhorrence hard to lull to rest.

He turned to grope; and I retiring brushed
    Thin shreds of gossamer from off my face,
And mused, His life would grow, the germ uncrushed;
    He should to antenatal night retrace,   70
And hide his elements in that large womb
Beyond the reach of man-evolving Doom.

And even thus, what weary way were planned,
    To seek oblivion through the far-off gate
Of birth, when that of death is close at hand!   75
    For this is law, if law there be in Fate:
What never has been, yet may have its when;
The thing which has been, never is again.

XIX

The mighty river flowing dark and deep,
   With ebb and flood from the remote sea-tides
Vague-sounding through the City's sleepless sleep,
   Is named the River of the Suicides;
For night by night some lorn wretch overweary,   5
And shuddering from the future yet more dreary,
   Within its cold secure oblivion hides.

One plunges from a bridge's parapet,
   As by some blind and sudden frenzy hurled;
Another wades in slow with purpose set   10
   Until the waters are above him furled;
Another in a boat with dreamlike motion
Glides drifting down into the desert ocean,
   To starve or sink from out the desert world.

They perish from their suffering surely thus,   15
   For none beholding them attempts to save,
The while each thinks how soon, solicitous,
   He may seek refuge in the self-same wave;
Some hour when tired of ever-vain endurance
Impatience will forerun the sweet assurance   20
   Of perfect peace eventual in the grave.

When this poor tragic-farce has palled us long,
　　Why actors and spectators do we stay? –
To fill our so-short *rôles* out right or wrong;
　　To see what shifts are yet in the dull play　　　　25
For our illusion; to refrain from grieving
Dear foolish friends by our untimely leaving:
　　But those asleep at home, how blest are they!

Yet it is but for one night after all:
　　What matters one brief night of dreary pain?　　　30
When after it the weary eyelids fall
　　Upon the weary eyes and wasted brain;
And all sad scenes and thoughts and feelings vanish
In that sweet sleep no power can ever banish,
　　That one best sleep which never wakes again.　　　35

X X

I sat me weary on a pillar's base,
    And leaned against the shaft; for broad moonlight
O'erflowed the peacefulness of cloistered space,
    A shore of shadow slanting from the right:
The great cathedral's western front stood there,   5
A wave-worn rock in that calm sea of air.

Before it, opposite my place of rest,
    Two figures faced each other, large, austere;
A couchant sphinx in shadow to the breast,
    An angel standing in the moonlight clear;   10
So mighty by magnificence of form,
They were not dwarfed beneath that mass enorm.

Upon the cross-hilt of a naked sword
    The angel's hands, as prompt to smite, were held;
His vigilant intense regard was poured   15
    Upon the creature placidly unquelled,
Whose front was set at level gaze which took
No heed of aught, a solemn trance-like look.

And as I pondered these opposèd shapes
    My eyelids sank in stupor, that dull swoon   20
Which drugs and with a leaden mantle drapes
    The outworn to worse weariness. But soon
A sharp and clashing noise the stillness broke,
And from the evil lethargy I woke.

The angel's wings had fallen, stone on stone,   25
    And lay there shattered; hence the sudden sound:
A warrior leaning on his sword alone
    Now watched the sphinx with that regard profound;
The sphinx unchanged looked forthright, as aware
Of nothing in the vast abyss of air.   30

Again I sank in that repose unsweet,
    Again a clashing noise my slumber rent;
The warrior's sword lay broken at his feet:
    An unarmed man with raised hands impotent
Now stood before the sphinx, which ever kept   35
Such mien as if with open eyes it slept.

My eyelids sank in spite of wonder grown;
    A louder crash upstartled me in dread:
The man had fallen forward, stone on stone,
    And lay there shattered, with his trunkless head   40
Between the monster's large quiscent paws,
Beneath its grand front changeless as life's laws.

The moon had circled westward full and bright,
    And made the temple-front a mystic dream,
And bathed the whole enclosure with its light,   45
    The sworded angel's wrecks, the sphinx supreme:
I pondered long that cold majestic face
Whose vision seemed of infinite void space.

XXI

Anear the centre of that northern crest
    Stands out a level upland bleak and bare,
From which the city east and south and west
    Sinks gently in long waves; and thronèd there
An Image sits, stupendous, superhuman,   5
The bronze colossus of a wingèd Woman,
    Upon a graded granite base foursquare.

Low-seated she leans forward massively,
    With cheek on clenched left hand, the forearm's might
Erect, its elbow on her rounded knee;   10
    Across a clasped book in her lap the right
Upholds a pair of compasses; she gazes
With full set eyes, but wandering in thick mazes
    Of sombre thought beholds no outward sight.

Words cannot picture her; but all men know   15
    That solemn sketch the pure sad artist wrought
Three centuries and threescore years ago,
    With phantasies of his peculiar thought:
The instruments of carpentry and science
Scattered about her feet, in strange alliance   20
    With the keen wolf-hound sleeping undistraught;

Scales, hour-glass, bell, and magic-square above;
    The grave and solid infant perched beside,
With open winglets that might bear a dove,
    Intent upon its tablets, heavy-eyed;   25
Her folded wings as of a mighty eagle,
But all too impotent to lift the regal
    Robustness of her earth-born strength and pride;

And with those wings, and that light wreath which seems
   To mock her grand head and the knotted frown   30
Of forehead charged with baleful thoughts and dreams,
   The household bunch of keys, the housewife's gown
Voluminous, indented, and yet rigid
As if a shell of burnished metal frigid,
   The feet thick-shod to tread all weakness down;   35

The comet hanging o'er the waste dark seas,
   The massy rainbow curved in front of it
Beyond the village with the masts and trees;
   The snaky imp, dog-headed, from the Pit,
Bearing upon its batlike leathern pinions   40
Her name unfolded in the sun's dominions,
   The 'MELENCOLIA' that transcends all wit.

Thus has the artist copied her, and thus
   Surrounded to expound her form sublime,
Her fate heroic and calamitous;   45
   Fronting the dreadful mysteries of Time,
Unvanquished in defeat and desolation,
Undaunted in the hopeless conflagration
   Of the day setting on her baffled prime.

Baffled and beaten back she works on still,   50
   Weary and sick of soul she works the more,
Sustained by her indomitable will:
   The hands shall fashion and the brain shall pore,
And all her sorrow shall be turned to labour,
Till Death the friend-foe piercing with his sabre   55
   That mighty heart of hearts ends bitter war.

But as if blacker night could dawn on night,
    With tenfold gloom on moonless night unstarred,
A sense more tragic than defeat and blight,
    More desperate than strife with hope debarred,   60
More fatal than the adamantine Never
Encompassing her passionate endeavour,
    Dawns glooming in her tenebrous regard:

The sense that every struggle brings defeat
    Because Fate holds no prize to crown success;   65
That all the oracles are dumb or cheat
    Because they have no secret to express;
That none can pierce the vast black veil uncertain
Because there is no light beyond the curtain;
    That all is vanity and nothingness.   70

Titanic from her high throne in the north,
    That City's sombre Patroness and Queen,
In bronze sublimity she gazes forth
    Over her Capital of teen and threne,
Over the river with its isles and bridges,   75
The marsh and moorland, to the stern rock-ridges,
    Confronting them with a coëval mien.

The moving moon and stars from east to west
    Circle before her in the sea of air;
Shadows and gleams glide round her solemn rest.   80
    Her subjects often gaze up to her there:
The strong to drink new strength of iron endurance,
The weak new terrors; all, renewed assurance
    And confirmation of the old despair.

Notes

i) Dante, *Inferno*, III.l.

'Through me is the way into the city of pain.' The first line of the nine-line inscription above the gate that leads into the hell of eternal pain (*eterno dolore*), the hell of the lost (*perduta gente*). Thomson taught himself Italian in order to read Dante in the original.

ii) Leopardi, '*Canti* XXIII: Canto notturno di un pastore errante dell'Asia', 93–98.

'Then out of such endless working, so many movements of everything in heaven and earth, revolving incessantly, only to return to the point from which they were moved: from all this I can imagine neither purpose nor gain.' This poem by Giacomo Leopardi (1798–1837) was suggested by a magazine article describing how nomadic Asiatic shepherds used to pass the night sitting on a rock, looking at the moon and improvising sad words and melancholy airs. The shepherd in the poem likens his wanderings to those of the moon and asks the moon and the stars if their great trajectories are more meaningful than his own transient existence. The shepherd's melancholy is also Leopardi's. Thomson's urban wanderer makes a third in the succession.

iii) Leopardi, *Operette Morali*, 'Coro di morti' from 'Dialogo di Federico Ruysch e delle sue mummie', 1–6, 31–32.

'Eternal alone in the world, receiver of all created things, in you, death, our naked being comes to rest; joyful no, but safe from the age-old pain ... For happiness is denied by fate to the living and denied to the dead.' This 'chorus of the dead' is a verse prologue to a prose dialogue in which Ruysch (1638–1731), a Dutch embalmer, interrogates his mummies about life and death. The poem is very grand in Leopardi's most uncompromising manner, and Thomson, who made his own verse translation of it, called it 'one of the marvels of literature'. Leopardi's *antico dolor* is the pain of life. Dante's *eterno dolore* is the pain of hell. Thomson's *dolorous mysteries* (Proem, 37) bridge both, with the idea of a hell on earth.

PROEM

1–2 Shakespeare, *Titus Andronicus*, III.i.12–13. Titus lies prostrate in the street, pleading desperately for the reprieve of his two sons, who are being led to execution. The judges and senators pass by without taking any notice – hence the 'careless ears' of line 7.

SECTION I

24 *Regurging* gushing back again.
78 Dante, *Inferno*, III.9: 'leave all hope behind, you who enter.'
84 The footnote appears to be by Thomson himself.

SECTION II

This section is reminiscent of Poe's story 'The Man of the Crowd' (1840), which is set in London.
10 *God's-acre* graveyard.
48 Thomson's footnote divides the three score years and ten of human life by the 'persistent three' terms of dead faith, dead love, and dead hope.

Notes

SECTION V

25 *dree his weird* endure his fate (Scots).

SECTION VI

37 In Greek mythology, the opening of Pandora's box unleashed all human misfortunes, though it is said that Hope remained in the box. Thomson seems to suggest the legend might someday be reversed, if sufficient hopes could be added to the box.

56 Theologically, Limbo is a borderline area or state set aside for those (such as virtuous pagans) who are not wicked enough for Hell but are not redeemed for Heaven.

SECTION VII

16 *Dead Sea foam* the biblical underpinning suggests Dead Sea fruit, sterility, disillusion. Thomson's distinction between the living who still have 'mysteries' and 'some inmost secret' and the living dead or zombies who are 'unsexed' and have gone beyond sexual guilt, seems a significant indicator in the poem.

SECTION XII

45 *great work* Milton's *Paradise Lost*.

SECTION XIV

31 *bale* misery.

65–66 Blake's poem 'The Tyger' was obviously in Thomson's mind. There are other Blakean echoes in this section, as also in Section XVIII.

SECTION XVIII

Ian Campbell has suggested an influence from Dante, *Inferno*, XV. The haggard old man dragging himself along the lane is reminiscent of Brunetto Latini who with his scorched face (*cotto aspetto*) looks up at the poet and seizes the hem of his gown. The (self-) torture is in both cases endless movement, endless restlessness. (See *Victorian Poetry*, XVI, 1978, p.127.)

4 *lown* sheltered (Scots).

SECTION XXI

16 *the pure sad artist* Albrecht Dürer (1471–1528), whose engraving *Melencolia I* is the 'solemn sketch' Thomson is about to describe.

22 *magic-square* a very ancient astrological device: the numbers in each line, whether taken horizontally, vertically, or diagonally, add up to the same total. In Dürer's engraving the square –

16	3	2	13
5	10	11	8
9	6	7	12
4	15	14	1

– has a double magic, since the four numerals in the inner square also add up to the same figure of 34. This figure, which at first sight seems not to mean very much, is in fact a quarter of the sum total of the numbers from 1 to 16, so emphasising the 'squareness' – and the 'magic'. The mathematician in Thomson must have relished these facts, and wondered whether that magic square portended any change of fate for Dürer's brooding woman.

63 *tenebrous* dark.

74 *teen and threne* affliction and lamentation.

Select Bibliography

Poems and Some Letters of James Thomson,
ed. A. Ridler, Centaur Press, London, 1963.

The Speedy Extinction of Evil and Misery: Selected Prose of James Thomson (B.V.), ed. W. D. Schaefer, University of California Press, Berkeley and Los Angeles, 1967.

James Thomson, *Essays and Phantasies,*
Reeves & Turner, London, 1881.

James Thomson, *Poems, Essays and Fragments,*
ed. J. M. Robertson, A. & H.B. Bonner, London, 1892.

The Poetical Works of James Thomson ('B.V.'),
ed. B. Dobell, 2 vols., Reeves & Turner & Dobell, London, 1895.

H. S. Salt, *The Life of James Thomson ('B.V.'),* Reeves & Turner & Dobell, London, 1889 (and later editions).

I. B. Walker, *James Thomson (B.V.): A Critical Study,* Cornell University Press, Ithaca, 1950.

W. D. Schaefer, *James Thomson (B.V.): Beyond 'The City',* University of California Press, Berkeley and Los Angeles, 1965.

T. Leonard, *Places of the Mind: The Life and Work of James Thomson ('B.V.'),* Cape, London, 1993.